Padma Shri Pran

Maurice Horn, the editor of World Encyclopedia of Comics, has described cartoonist PRAN as Walt Disney of India.

Entertaining generation after generation, his comics have been constant companion of all the growing youngsters providing fun and amusement through his famous characters like CHACHA CHAUDHARY, SABU, SHRIMATIJI, PINKI, BILLOO, RAMAN etc. More than 600 of his titles are selling well in the market, and numerous comic strips are regularly appearing in various newspapers. His CHACHA CHAUDHARY comics had already been adapted for a TV Serial, and ran continuously for 600 episodes on a premier channel.

Travelling widely over the globe, he delivers lectures at various International Conferences. He has also been honoured with 'People of The Year Award' by Limca Book of Records for popularizing comics. His comic book 'United We Stand' was released in 1983 by the then Prime Minister Mrs. Indira Gandhi, and is still very popular among children.

Publisher

4

7

HE'S THE MAIN CONSPIRATOR! HIS BUYING COSTLY JEWELLERY WITHIN FEW DAYS AROSE MY SUSPICION!

WHEN I CHECKED THE ACCOUNTS OF PETROL COMPANY, I FOUND THE SAME NUMBERS OF NOTES ENTERED IN COMPUTER, WITH WHICH RULROULLA MADE PAYMENTS FOR JEWELLERY HE BOUGHT! HE EVEN DID NOT TAKE SECURITY MAN THAT DAY!

THEN WHY DID THE CULPRITS HIT AND WOUNDED HIM?

THAT WAS ONLY A DRAMA! HIS HEAD HAS NO INJURY!

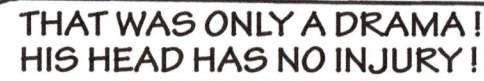

THIS ROD IS LIGHT AND HOLLOW PLASTIC!

AND HERE ARE THEIR MASKS! THE THREE DISTRIBUTED THE LOOT AMONG THEMSELVES.

CHACHA CHAUDHARY'S BRAIN WORKS FASTER THAN COMPUTER.

COCKROACH

11

RUN OUTSIDE!

WHERE WOULD YOU GO?

WHAM!!

BINI! ALL COCKROCHES HAVE BEEN KILLED!

NOW I HAVE TO SWEEP THEIR CORPSES!

RAAHU HAS SENT FOR BOTH OF YOU!

IT'S A PRIVATE GARDEN! NO ONE IS ALLOWED TO ENTER!

SIR! WE APOLOGIES! IN FACT WE STRAYED IN!

BOY! YOU'RE EXCUSED! YOU CAN GO! GIRL WILL STAY HERE!

?!

15

PASSWORD

FRIEND RAHUL! WHY'RE YOU TENSE?

GOLDY! I'VE LOST FIVE LAC RUPEES IN A CASINO!

PLEASE LEND ME MONEY WHICH I HAVE TO PAY SOMEONE!

I DON'T HAVE THAT MUCH AMOUNT!

BORROW FROM YOUR DAD!

THAT MISER WOULD NOT PAY A SINGLE RUPEE, EVEN IF I AM KIDNAPPED!

23

A SERVANT EMERGES...

25

SMART AND SMARTER

SABU ! YOU HAVE LONG LEGS AND ROCKET CAN RUN FASTER THAN I CAN ! STILL YOU TWO REMAIN BEHIND ME ?

WE DO THAT DUE TO REVERENCE TO YOU !

OR IF ANY TROUBLE COMES ON WAY, I WOULD BE THE FIRST TO FACE THAT !

YOU ARE TRAPPED !

RUN !

BOW ! BOW !!

OHH ! WHAT THE HELL IS THIS ?

?!

I BROUGHT OUT MONEY SLOWLY TO GIVE TIME TO MY COLLEAGUES TO REACH HERE !

CHACHA CHAUDHARY'S BRAIN WORKS FASTER THAN COMPUTER.

31

CAT AND DOG

AAAAWWSS !

ROCKET ! YAWNING IS THE SIGN OF LAZINESS !

GO AND RUN TO SEVEN OR EIGHT KILOMETRES. THAT WOULD MAKE YOU ALERT !

RUN FAST ! IMAGINE THERE IS A BOWL OF MILK AHEAD !

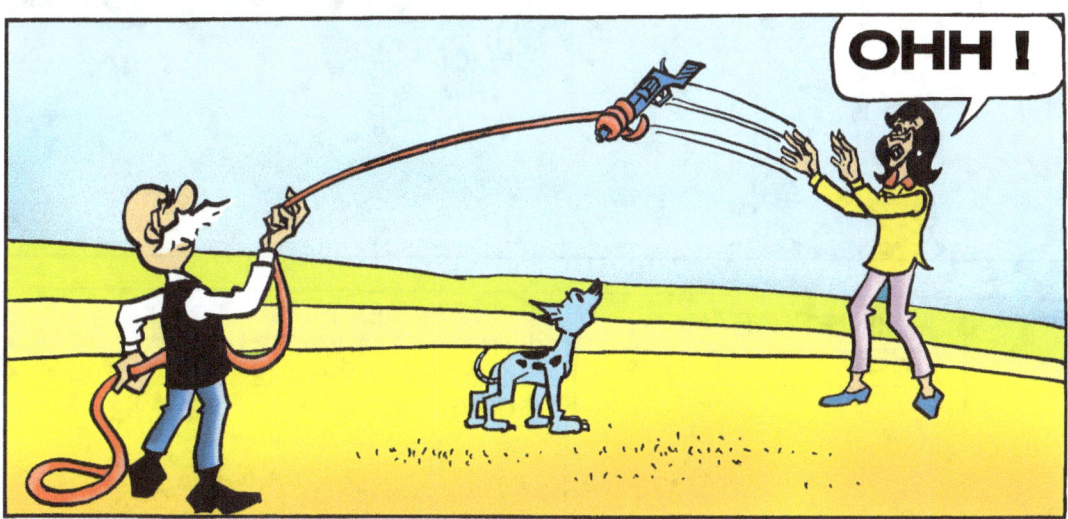

35

PUZZLE

OHH! I AM THIRSTY, BUT NO WATER IN PITCHER!

TODAY THERE IS NO WATER IN TAPS!

MINISTER SAHEB! THERE IS SHORTAGE OF WATER IN CITY! WHAT ARE YOU DOING?

I'VE INCREASED THE RATE OF WATER! COSTLY THINGS ARE CONSUMED LESS!

39

41

ADULTERATED MILK

WHERE'RE YOU GOING ?

THERE'S A NEW DAIRY ! THEY GIVE HALF A LITRE MILK FREE ON BUYING TWO LITRES !

THAT MUST BE ADULTERATED !

NO ! IT IS CREAMY !

I'LL GET MORE AT SAME PRICE !

43

www.chachachaudhry.com

WHITE POWDER, SHAMPOO AND REFIND OIL?

SO THEY MAKE SUB-STANDARD MILK HERE!

HELLO! POLICE?

DAWN.

FOOD INSPECTOR! HERE'S THE OWNER OF DAIRY!

I BROUGHT A POLYPACK MILK! I'LL MAKE COFFEE FOR BOTH OF US!

TASTE

© PRAN'S FEATURES

CHACHA CHAUDHARY™
FOOTBALL WORLD CUP

WOW !

HOW COME YOU ARE HAPPY TODAY ?

I AND SABU HAVE BEEN INVITED TO **FOOTBALL WORLD CUP TOURNAMENT !**

BINI ! PACK OUR CLOTHES AND BELONGINGS !

50

53

BIOGRAPHY

CHACHI ! HAPPY BIRTHDAY TO YOU !

THANK YOU !

DON'T KNOW, WHETHER YOUR CHACHAJI REMEMBERS TODAY'S DAY OR NOT ?

AHA ! I HAVE REACHED HOME!

© PRAN'S FEATURES

WWW.CHACHACHAUDHARY.COM

56

TIT FOR TAT

A SPACECRAFT PROCEEDES TOWARDS EARTH.

TWO ALIENS, LAKAR AND BAKAR BROTHERS EMERGE FROM IT.

WWW.CHACHACHAUDHARY.COM

LAKAR! WE HAVE TO CONQUER THE EARTHLINGS!

BAKAR! SHOW THEM YOUR MIGHT!

© PRAN'S FEATURES

63

CHACHA CHAUDHARY™
FAKE CURRENCY

© PRAN'S FEATURES

SUDDENLY CAR OWNER'S PHONE STARTED RINGING !

WHAT ? YOU WANTED TO STEAL MY MOBILE ?

THAT GENTLEMAN ACTUALLY TURNED OUT TO BE A SUPERINTENDENT OF POLICE !

HA!-- HA!!

CHACHA CHAUDHARY ! A LADY SWINDLED ME AND GAVE THREE FAKE NOTES OF ONE THOUSAND RUPEES EACH !

CHACHA CHAUDHARY'S BRAIN WORKS FASTER THAN COMPUTER.

69

WHAT IS THIS JOKE, CHAUDHARY ?
THE PAPER IS BLANK ?

HA! HA!!

FOOL ! THAT WAS A MISS CALL FOR TRIAL !

THIS TIME THE PIGEON IS TAKING A MESSAGE !

GULGUL- BIRD HUNTER—

THIS IS BRINGING CHACHA CHAUDHARY'S MESSAGE ! LET ME HUNT IT !

PRINCESS HOLLYWOOD

VIRUS! ARE YOU WATCHING A HOLLYWOOD MOVIE ON COMPUTER?

STUNTS OF THIS HERO ARE GOOD!

IT IS NOT A FILM, BUT TRUE ACTION!

HE IS **SABU**, COMPANION OF CHACHA CHAUDHARY!

HE CAN BE USEFUL TO US!

IF HE WILL BE THE HERO OF A FILM, THAT WILL BE A SUPER HIT!

MY DAD IS A PRODUCER! HE'LL PRODUCE AN ACTION FILM! AND CAST ME AS THE HEROINE AND SABU AS AN ACTION HERO!

TO SIGN HIM, WE'LL HAVE TO GO TO CHACHA CHAUDHARY!

LET THE WORLD BE HAPPY

79

FISH FROM SKY

CHACHI! IT'S A HOT DAY! IF WE GET *LASSI*, THEN IT WILL COOL OUR THROATS.

TAKE A DIP IN THE RIVER, YOUR WHOLE BODY WILL COOL DOWN!

CHACHAJI! WHERE ARE YOU GOING? RIVER IS ON THE OPPOSITE SIDE!

THAT RIVER IS DRIED UP BY MINERAL WATER COMPANIES. WE WILL HAVE TO GO TO THE SEA!

84

HUMOUR

86

WHAT IS LOVE?

91

93

Help the puzzle piece to find the way to the puzzle.

Draw a line from dot number 1 to dot number 2, then from dot number 2 to dot number 3, 3 to 4, and so on. Continue to join the dots until you have connected all the numbered dots. Then color the picture!

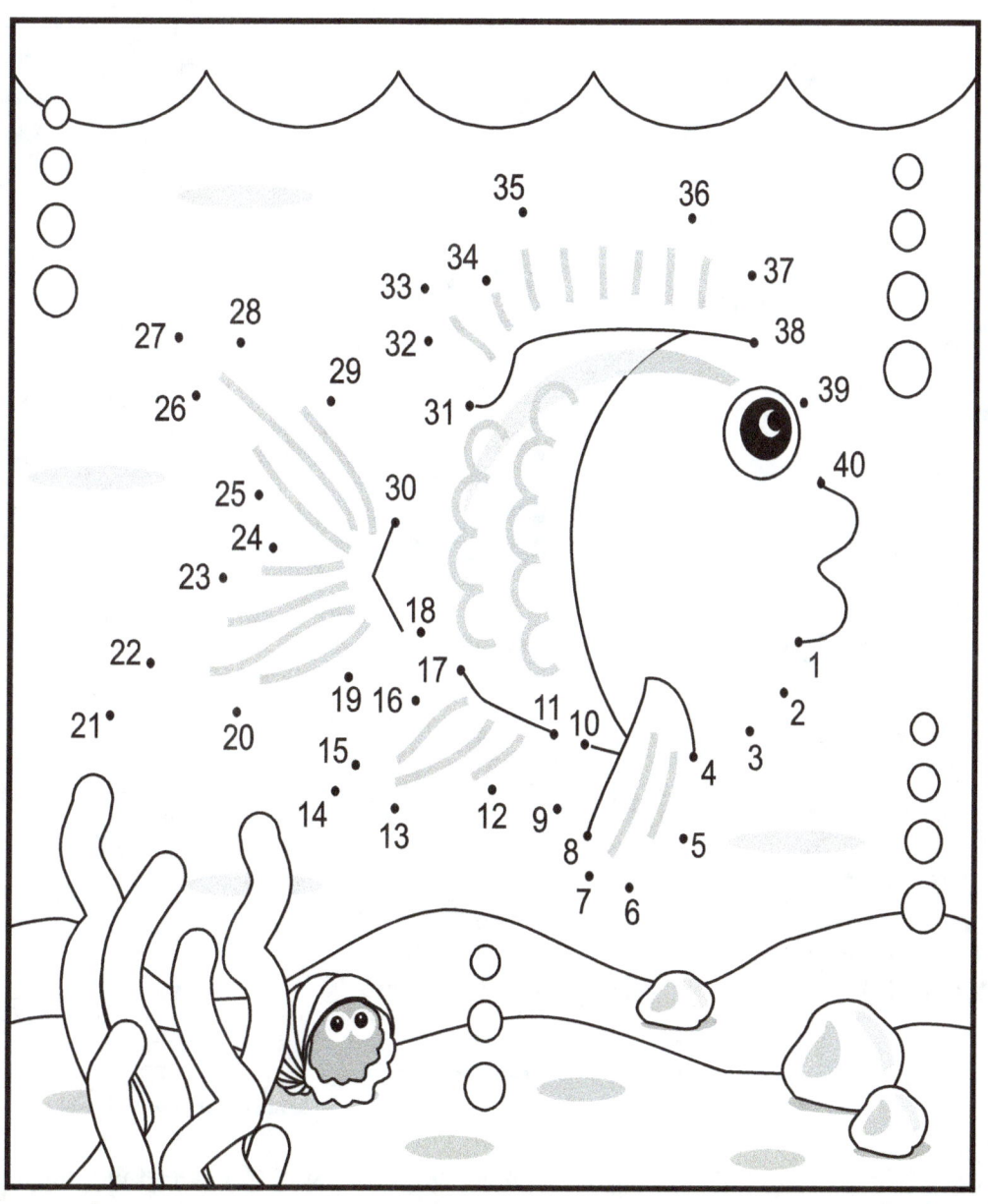

Draw a line from dot number 1 to dot number 2, then from dot number 2 to dot number 3, 3 to 4, and so on. Continue to join the dots until you have connected all the numbered dots. Then color the picture!

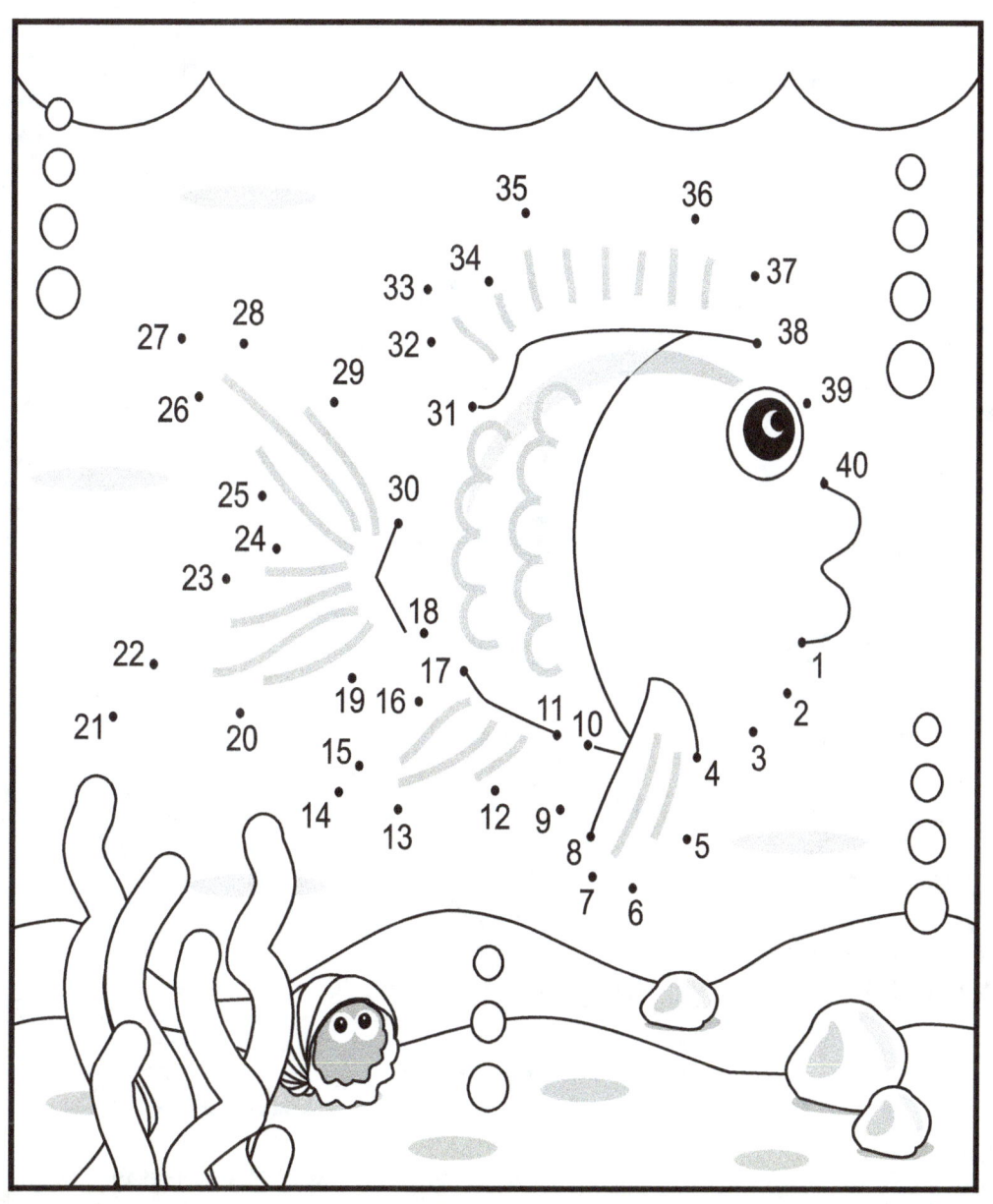

     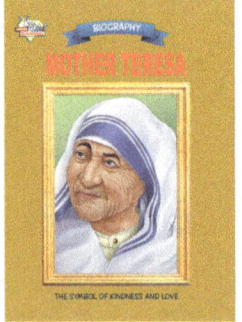 

www.ingramcontent.com/pod-product-compliance
Lightning Source LLC
Chambersburg PA
CBHW080733020726
47503CB00010B/2900